To Rob
Love, Pop Pop & Rosalie
Jan. "2013"

This edition published by Parragon in 2009

Parragon
Queen Street House
4 Queen Street
Bath BA1 1HE, UK

ISBN 978-1-4075-8364-8
Printed in China

Barnyard stories

Bath · New York · Singapore · Hong Kong · Cologne · Delhi · Melbourne

Sleepy the Farm Kitten

Sleepy the farm kitten liked nothing better than sleeping all day long, and all through the night. While all the other kittens were busy chasing mice or scaring away birds, he was usually fast asleep.

"Looks too much like hard work to me," he'd yawn, before strolling off to find a comfy spot for a snooze.

One day, while the other kittens were chasing mice around the barns, Sleepy stretched and looked around for somewhere to nap.

"You can't sleep here," said the farmer's wife, sweeping Sleepy out of the kitchen. "Today's cleaning day and you'll just be in the way."

"You can't sleep here," mooed the cows, shooing him out of the milking parlor. "We're busy being milked, and a kitten can never be trusted around milk."

"You can't sleep here," said the farmer, pushing him out of the dairy. "We're making ice cream and we don't want your hairs all over the place."

"I'm really tired," Sleepy complained to a passing mouse. "Can I sleep with you mice?"

"Don't be ridiculous," laughed the mouse. "Don't you know that kittens are supposed to chase mice?"

Just as Sleepy was about to give up hope of ever finding somewhere to sleep, he spotted the ideal bed—a soft bale of hay sitting on a trailer.

"Purrfect," he purred, curling into a sleepy ball. Within seconds, he was fast asleep.

He was so comfortable that he didn't wake up when the tractor pulling the trailer chugged into life. And he still didn't wake up when the tractor and trailer bumped down the road leading to town.

It was only when the trailer shuddered to a halt that Sleepy woke with a start. He blinked his eyes, stretched, and jumped down. Then he blinked again. He couldn't believe his eyes! He was at a market—and the farmer had unhitched the trailer and was driving away in the tractor.

"Wait for me," mewed Sleepy, leaping down from the trailer. But the farmer was gone.

"I'll have to walk all the way home," thought Sleepy.

Sleepy walked all afternoon and all through the night. The rooster was just beginning to crow the morning in when he eventually made it back to the farm.

"Hello, lazybones," called the other kittens when they saw him. "Where have you been sleeping all night while we've been chasing mice?"

But for once Sleepy really was tired—much too tired to explain where he had been all night. And it wasn't long before he was fast asleep!

A Hat Like That

Heather the cow took good care of her appearance. She had the shiniest hoofs and the glossiest coat. She had already won three ribbons at the County Fair, and she wanted more.

One windy afternoon, when Heather was standing near a hedge, she found a beautiful straw hat on a branch. It had a couple of holes in it, but an elegant cow has to put her ears somewhere!

She strolled back across the field with her nose in the air and the hat placed firmly on her head. Heather couldn't wait to show it off to her friends.

But Poppy, Annabel, and Emily simply kept on munching. Heather tried a tiny ladylike cough.

The munching didn't stop for a second. So Heather coughed a little louder. The munching grew louder.

Heather couldn't bear it any longer. "Haven't you noticed it?" she mooed.

"Did I hear something?" asked Emily.

"It was me!" cried Heather, stamping her hoof angrily. "Look at my hat!"

Of course, the other cows had noticed the hat, but they loved to tease their friend.

"I always think,"

said Poppy, "that hats are rather… old-fashioned."

"Nonsense," Heather replied. "Only the most fashionable cows are wearing them."

"So new, then is it?" asked Annabel.

"Certainly!" Heather replied. "It's the very latest style."

"Didn't Mrs. MacDonald have a hat like that a few years ago?" asked Emily.

"I don't think so!" Heather said firmly. "Mrs. MacDonald is lovely, but she's not what you would call stylish. Only a prize-winning cow could wear a hat like this."

"If you say so, dear," mooed Annabel.

That evening, the cows ambled into the barnyard to be milked.

Before long, all the other animals had gathered around.

"They're admiring my hat!" whispered Heather to Poppy.

But the giggling and chuckling didn't sound as if they thought Heather looked beautiful. It sounded more like animals who thought she looked a little silly.

"Well, well! So that's what happened to Scarecrow Sam's hat!" cried Old MacDonald.

So nowadays, if Heather starts putting on airs, Poppy, Emily and Annabel know just what to do—they start talking about hats, and Heather tiptoes away.

Missing Milk

One day, Farmer Fred was feeling very pleased with himself.

"I don't like to boast," he told his wife Jenny, "but I'm sure my singing is doing Connie Cow a world of good. She's grown very plump around the middle. And she's giving me buckets of milk."

Jenny looked at Connie. "Do you suppose she could be…?"

But Farmer Fred was too busy singing to listen.

The next day, as Connie waddled toward the milking parlor, the other farm animals gossiped amongst themselves.

"I'm sure she's getting fatter," clucked Hetty Hen.

"You don't think she's having a baby, do you?" asked Harry Horse. The animals began to chatter excitedly with one another.

A week later, Farmer Fred wasn't feeling so pleased.

"Connie's run out of milk," he moaned. "Maybe I'm singing the wrong songs." He closed his eyes and burst into song. Connie mooed loudly. She wished Farmer Fred would be quieter.

"I just don't understand it," said Farmer Fred. "Where has her milk gone?"

The animals tried to tell Farmer Fred that Connie had a new calf who was drinking all Connie's milk. But Farmer Fred just looked puzzled at all the noise.

"He just doesn't understand," sighed Harry Horse, knocking over the bucket with his hoof. Farmer Fred's eyes lit up.

"Yes, that's got to be it! There's a milk thief on the farm!" cried Farmer Fred. "But never fear, I have an idea!"

Farmer Fred disappeared into his workshop. There were sounds of drawers opening and closing, and cupboard doors banging.

All the animals wondered what was happening.

"What's Farmer Fred up to now?" asked Polly Pig.

Finally, Farmer Fred came out holding a large ball of string that he had found.

"I'm going to set a trap to catch that milk thief," he said. Farmer Fred got a really long piece of string and tied one end to the gate leading to Cowslip Meadow.

When Farmer Fred went to bed that night, he tied the other end of the string to his big toe.

He had only been sleeping for a few minutes when he felt a tug on his big toe.

"Thundering turnips!" grunted Farmer Fred, hopping out of bed. He peered through the window. But it was only an owl perching on the string.

11

"Get off my string!" he shouted.

Soon there was so much noise that everyone woke up.

The next morning, everyone on the farm was very, very tired. Hetty Hen called a barnyard meeting. Everyone but Connie was there.

"It's time Farmer Fred found out the truth about Connie. Otherwise we'll never get any peace around here," yawned Hetty Hen.

"Patch, it's up to you," neighed Harry Horse. "Farmer Fred always listens to you."

That night, Farmer Fred stood guard with his pitchfork in Cowslip Meadow.

"No one's going to get away with stealing my milk," he muttered.

Very slowly, and very carefully, he began counting the cows.

"One, two, yawn…" All this counting was making him sleepy. "Three, four, yawn… zzzz." He was fast asleep before he'd even reached five. But Patch wasn't going to let Farmer Fred snooze the night away.

"Woof, woof!" he barked.

"What? Where?" cried Farmer Fred, suddenly waking up.

"Woof, woof!" Patch scampered across the field barking over his shoulder at Farmer Fred.

"Do you want me to follow you, Patch?" asked Farmer Fred sleepily. "Have you found that milk thief?"

Patch led Farmer Fred to the old barn at the top of the field.

Farmer Fred shone his flashlight around the barn. And there in the corner was Connie. Beside her was the milk thief—a beautiful baby calf.

"Aah! You've got a little calf to feed!" cried Farmer Fred. "No wonder you had no milk to spare, Connie!"

The next day, Farmer Fred was feeling very pleased with himself.

"I don't like to boast," Farmer Fred told Jenny, "but I just knew Connie was going to have a calf. After all, she was looking very plump!"

Jenny and Patch looked at each other and rolled their eyes.

Harry, Hetty, Polly, Shirley, and all the other animals smiled happily. Now maybe they could all get some sleep!

Maria's Haircut

One spring day, Maria the sheep stood by the pond in Old MacDonald's barnyard, gazing sadly into the water.

"What is she doing?" whispered Doris the duck to her friend Dora. "You don't often see sheep near water."

Meanwhile, ducklings were swimming across to see who the visitor was.

"Sheep don't eat ducklings, do they?" asked Dora anxiously.

"Of course not!" replied Doris.

Just then, Maria gave such a big sigh that she blew the ducklings right across the pond and they had to be rescued by their mothers!

"What's the trouble, my dear?" asked Old George, the horse. "Has your lamb run away again?"

"No," sighed Maria. "It isn't that. Just look at me!"

Old George looked carefully at Maria. "Well, you look even more, um, wonderfully woolly than usual," he said gallantly.

"I look terrible," said Maria. "My coat should have been trimmed weeks ago, but Old MacDonald seems to have forgotten."

"Hmmmm. He can be a little forgetful," said Old George. "I'll speak to the other animals and see what they suggest."

"Maybe I could nibble her coat," said Percy the pig, who would eat almost anything!

"No, we need to remind Old MacDonald to give Maria a haircut," said Poppy the cow.

"Old MacDonald is always so busy," added Henrietta the hen. "How can we make him notice Maria's problem?"

That gave Poppy a very good idea.

"It's Mrs. MacDonald who notices things," she mooed thoughtfully. "Maybe you *should* do some nibbling, Percy!"

So Percy did a little nibbling and the hens scurried away with the tufts of wool in their beaks, searching for the farmer.

When Old MacDonald went into the farmhouse for his lunch that day, Mrs. MacDonald threw up her hands in horror! "MacD!" she cried. "You're covered with wool! Don't bring all that fluff into my clean kitchen! It's obviously time those sheep were shorn."

The very next day, Maria's haircut was the talk of the barnyard. And she and her friends strutted happily around, looking as elegant and as stylish as any sheep you've ever seen.

Slow Down, Bruce

On Old MacDonald's farm, no one works harder
than Bruce the farm dog—except, of course,
Old MacDonald! All day long, Bruce
dashes around the farm, keeping an eye on
everything that goes on. So, when Bruce
stayed in his doghouse one morning
with his head on his paws, everyone began
to worry.

"It's not like him at all," clucked Henrietta
the hen.

"He can hardly open his eyes," purred Milly the cat.

"I don't think he's ever had a day's illness in his life," said
Old George the horse, "and I remember him as a pup."

Old MacDonald was more worried than any of them.

"Just stay there, old boy," he said gently. "I'll get someone
to help you." And he hurried off to call the vet.

The vet arrived very quickly. She too was very fond of Bruce.

She carefully examined him, lifting his paws one by one,
and checking every part of him thoroughly. Then she patted

the old dog's head and said, "You're like your master. You need to stop dashing around so much and take better care of yourself. You'll be fine in a day or two, but just slow down, Bruce. Take it easy for once, please."

Bruce nodded his head gratefully and went back to sleep.

Now, Mrs. MacDonald had been listening, and returned to the farmhouse with a thoughtful look on her face.

Bruce did as he was told, and by the end of the week he was as right as rain—soon it would be time to go back to work.

When he saw Old MacDonald rushing through the yard, hurrying to finish a job, Bruce dashed after him.

But Mrs. MacDonald rushed out of the farmhouse and called to the farmer.

"Husband!" she cried. "Did you hear what the vet said about Bruce? You must set a good example for him! Please be a little more thoughtful!"

So Old MacDonald began to slow down, and so did Bruce. The dog soon felt better—and so did Old MacDonald. And Mrs. MacDonald, who had been begging her husband to take it easy for years, felt happiest of all.

Small and Pink

One morning, Percy the pig strutted proudly through the barnyard.

"Today's the day," he told everyone he passed.

"What is he talking about?" asked Doris the duck.

"Percy is expecting some piglets," clucked Jenny the hen.

"I didn't think boy pigs could have babies," said Doris, looking puzzled.

"No, no," Jenny clucked, flapping her wings. "They are coming from another farm to live here as part of his family."

Percy had tripped and trotted from one end of the barnyard to the other more times than he could remember, but Farmer Brown still hadn't returned with the new arrivals.

Percy went back to his sty and checked it one more time. It was spotless. The straw was piled up neatly along one wall and the water trough was clean and full.

"I must make sure that everything is ready for my piglets," said Percy, brushing a speck of dust from the doorway.

Just as Percy finished cleaning, brushing, and tidying he heard Farmer Brown's truck rumbling into the barnyard—they were here at last!

Percy was so excited! He hurried from his sty, but before he could reach the truck...

Whoosh! Something very small, very pink, and very fast shot past his nose.

Whizzz! Something just as small and pink and even faster

scuttled under his tail.

Wheeeee! Another small and pink and noisy thing zoomed straight under Percy's tummy.

"*Eeeeeeeeee!*" shrieked seven little piglets, dashing in every direction around the barnyard.

Late that night, a very tired Percy stood at the doorway of his sty—it was a mess. The straw was everywhere and the water trough was upside down. But seven little piglets were fast asleep in the corner.

"They never stand still, do they?" said Jasmine the sheep.

"No," sighed Percy.

"Are you having second thoughts, Percy?" asked Old Harry the horse.

But Percy gave the kind of grin that only a very happy, contented, and proud pig can give. "*Shhhhhhh!*" he whispered. "My babies are sleeping!"

The Rainy Day

Rain! It splashed on the windows, gurgled down the drainpipes, and made puddles all over the yard. And Danny and Rosie were bored. Bored, bored, bored!

Out in the pigsty, Bessie and her piglets wallowed in a giant mud bath. It was so much fun! There were squeals of delight.

On the pond, the ducks bobbed along, looking pleased with themselves. Rain was just water off a duck's back!

Down by the bridge, the river was rising higher and higher. Eventually, it spilled over its banks and brown muddy water flowed across the road and under the farm gate.

Joe was busy fixing the tractor in the barn when he heard a shout from the road and saw Jack the mail carrier struggling through the water on his bike.

"Help, Joe! I'm stranded!" called Jack.

"Don't worry, Jack," Joe shouted back. "We'll get you across."

Joe put down his tools and climbed up into the tractor cab. He started the engine and reversed out of the barn.

Rosie and Danny came out of the house in their rain slickers and ran down to the bridge with Ginger the dog.

"Look," gasped Rosie. "The ducklings are swimming all over the garden. And Jack's trapped by the flood!"

Joe rumbled up in the tractor. "Get on the trailer," he shouted to the children. "I'll reverse it through the flood."

"Nice weather for ducks," puffed Jack, as he scrambled aboard. "Thanks, kids. Oh, no! There goes my cap!"

Ginger barked wildly and jumped in after it.

"Come back, Ginger," cried Rosie. "You'll be swept away!"

"No he won't, silly," said Danny. "Ginger's a champion swimmer. Go fetch it, girl!"

Ginger grabbed the mail carrier's cap in her mouth, and paddled back to the trailer. She dropped it and wagged her tail.

"Good old Ginger!" shouted everyone. "Good job, girl!" Ginger shook herself furiously, spraying them all with water.

Joe drove back to the yard and they all jumped off

the trailer.

"Thank you, everyone," said Jack, picking up his cap. "Especially you, Ginger. I'm very fond of this old cap."

"Come inside," called Mom. "You're all soaking wet. And there's been so much excitement for a wet Tuesday morning!"

"Brave dog," said Danny, giving Ginger a pat.

The Farm Show

Farmer Jones was very excited. It was the day of the Sunnybridge Farm Show.

Mrs. Jones was entering the Jam-making Competition, and Farmer Jones was entering almost everything else.

"Maybe you should just enter one thing," said Mrs. Jones.

"But there are so many prizes to win," laughed Farmer Jones. "How could I possibly choose? Right, Max?"

Max, Farmer Jones's sheepdog, wagged his tail. He was looking forward to the Farm Show too.

"Pansy is sure to win the Prettiest Pig event," said Farmer Jones, as he and Max made their way to the pigsty where Pansy lived.

But Pansy had been rolling in something very dirty and very smelly.

"Phew!" gasped Farmer Jones.

"Woof!" barked Max, running back to the farmhouse to get some of Mrs. Jones's extra-strong laundry soap. Farmer Jones used the soap to make a bath.

But it was no use. Pansy was just too dirty and too smelly. They would never get her clean in time.

"Fiddlesticks! It doesn't look like I'll be winning the prize for the Prettiest Pig this year," said Farmer Jones. "But Bonnie is sure to win the prize for the Snowiest Lamb."

Farmer Jones borrowed some of Mrs. Jones's best shampoo and made a bath for Bonnie.

"In you go!" he said, plonking Bonnie into the tub. Farmer Jones began to scrub. He closed his eyes and began to sing:

"Oh, what a beautiful morning!
Oh, what a beautiful day!
I have a wonderful feeling
I'll win some prizes today!"

"Woof!" barked Max. He tugged at Farmer Jones's sleeve.

"What is it?" asked Farmer Jones.

But it was too late. Bonnie was bright pink.

Farmer Jones had picked up Mrs. Jones's hair dye instead of shampoo!

"Blast!" said Farmer Jones. "It doesn't look like I'll be winning the prize for the Snowiest Lamb this year. But Chloe is sure to win the prize for the Best-looking Cow."

Max brought Chloe from the meadow. Farmer Jones tied her up and found a brush.

"We'll soon have you gleaming," said Farmer Jones. But Chloe had other ideas. As soon as the brush touched her side, she began to wriggle and squirm.

Farmer Jones had forgotten that Chloe was ticklish! Chloe would not stand still. She would never be ready in time.

"Botheration!" said Farmer Jones. "Now what am I going to do?"

"Are you ready?" shouted Mrs. Jones from the farmhouse. "I don't want to be late for the Jam-making Competition."

"Double botheration!" said Farmer Jones. "I've run out of time. It doesn't look like I'll be entering any of the competitions this year."

Later, at Sunnybridge Farm Show, Mrs. Jones won first prize in the Jam-making Competition.

Farmer Jones watched as other farmers won the rest

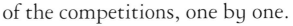

of the competitions, one by one.

"Oh, if only I could enter just one little competition," said Farmer Jones.

"Woof!" barked Max. He ran around in circles pretending to round up some invisible animals.

Suddenly, Farmer Jones understood. "Of course! The Sheepdog Competition," he said.

A few minutes later, they were in the ring. Farmer Jones whistled and Max herded the sheep this way and that. The sheep were herded into the pen in record time.

"And the winners are Farmer Jones and Max," said a voice over the loudspeaker. The crowd clapped and cheered.

Later, Farmer Jones showed Mrs. Jones the shiny cup they had won.

"It's like I always say," said Farmer Jones happily. "It's best to concentrate on just one thing."

Mrs. Jones peered over the cup she had won for her jam.

"Yes, dear," she said, winking at Max.

A Friend for Barney

It was Saturday morning at Primrose Farm. Robbie, Jenny, and Marley the dog went down to the pond to feed some breadcrumbs to the ducks.

"All the ducks are friends," said Jenny. "They never fight about who gets the biggest piece."

"Not like you," said Robbie.

"That's because you always get the biggest piece," said Jenny.

When they went to see the chickens, Robbie asked, "Are they friends too?"

"I think so," said Jenny, "but some of them get a little pecky."

"What about the pigs? Sometimes Bessie gets grumpy with her piglets," said Robbie.

"Oh, that's just because she is their mom," said Jenny. "They are very greedy sometimes, so Bessie has to scold them."

"Everybody at Primrose Farm has friends," agreed Robbie.

"My best friend is Stanley," said Jenny.

"Cats are boring," declared Robbie. "They just sleep all the time. My best friend is Marley. He's the fastest dog in the world!"

"But Barney the scarecrow

doesn't have a friend," said Jenny, frowning. "He just stands on the hill all day with no one to talk to."

When they went back to the house, Jenny said to her mom, "Barney's lonely."

"Then why don't you make him a friend?" asked Mom. That afternoon she took them to a rummage sale in town so they could get some clothes for a new scarecrow. Robbie found an old pair of sneakers and a pair of motorbike gloves. Jenny found a pink party dress and a hat with a green ribbon.

Robbie stuffed an old sack with straw and Dad helped Jenny paint a face at the top. Mom made some hair out of yarn.

"What a beauty," said Dad. "All she needs is a name."

"I want to call her Mary, like my favorite doll," said Jenny.

"Scary Mary Crow," said Robbie. "That's a great name."

So that's what they called her. They took Scary Mary up the hill.

"Hello, Barney," said Robbie. "We've brought you a friend."

"Now you won't be lonely anymore," added Jenny.

"I think Barney likes her," said Robbie. "He can see by looking at the shoes she's wearing that she's very good at sports."

"I think he likes her because she has a smiley face," said Jenny.

Jenny skipped all the way home to tell Stanley the cat all about Scary Mary. "I'm very happy, Stanley," she said, giving him a big hug. "Now everybody at Primrose Farm has a friend."

Nibbling Neighbors

One sunny morning in the meadow, Alice was happily munching when she was surprised to discover a hole where there should be grass.

"My dears," she mooed, "there's a hole in our field!"

The next morning, where there had been one hole before, now there were five!

"If this goes on," said Daisy, "we'll have nowhere to stand!"

"And nothing to eat," added Clarissa, sounding alarmed.

By the end of the week, there were over a hundred holes.

"You've got some nibbling neighbors," said Farmer Jim. "It looks like a family of rabbits has come to stay."

The cows shuddered. "Those hopping things with long ears?" asked Mabel. "I can't look my best with them around!"

"And they have very, very large families," warned Clarissa. "Not just one baby at a time, like cows do."

"It's odd that we've never seen one," said Daisy thoughtfully. "I'm going to keep watch tonight."

That night, as the full moon rose over the meadow, Daisy pretended to go to sleep. Although she was expecting it, she was shocked when two bright eyes and a twitchy nose popped up in front of her.

"*Aaaaaghh!*" cried Daisy.

"*Aaaaaghh!*" cried the rabbit, and disappeared down its hole.

"You should have followed it!" cried Alice, who had been woken by the sudden noise.

"Down a rabbit hole?" gasped Clarissa. "Don't be silly, Alice. She's much too big!"

"Then we're doomed," said Mabel gloomily. "Those rabbits will take over without us even seeing them do it."

The next morning, the cows awoke to an amazing sight. Hundreds of rabbits were sitting around them.

"Excuse me!" said the largest one. "We've come to ask for your help."

"Help?" echoed Alice. "We're the ones who need help!"

The rabbit explained that his family lived in fear. "Your hoofs are so big, you could stamp on us without noticing."

Just then, Daisy had one of her excellent ideas. "You would be much safer," she said, "if you lived under the hedges."

So they did. All day in the meadow, there's munching and mooing. All night in the hedges, there's nibbling, digging, and wiggling. And everyone is happy.